THE BANSHEE TRAIN

by Odds Bodkin/Illustrated by Ted Rose

CLARION BOOKS • NEW YORK

Clarion Books
a Houghton Mifflin Company imprint
215 Park Avenue South, New York, NY 10003
Text copyright © 1995 by Odds Bodkin
Illustrations copyright © 1995 by Ted Rose
Illustrations executed in watercolor on Arches paper.
Type is 14-pt. ITC Cheltenham
Printed in Singapore.

Library of Congress Cataloging-in-Publication Data
Bodkin, Odds.
The Banshee train / by Odds Bodkin ; illustrated by Ted Rose.
p. cm.
Summary: In the mountains outside of Denver, a passenger train is saved from
certain disaster by the ghosts from a previous wreck.
ISBN 0-395-69426-4
[1. Railroad accidents—Fiction. 2. Ghosts—Fiction.] I. Rose, Ted, ill. II. Title.
PZ7.B6355Ban 1995
[E]—dc20 93-39635
CIP AC

*To John and Eleanor Bodkin, who once in Canada
took a small boy on a railroad adventure.*
—O.B.

————————

To Kent, Gil, Howard, and George.
—T.R.

In the spring of 1929, a strange event took place in the mountains west of Denver, Colorado. Although Train Number 1 to Troublesome and Steamboat Springs was filled with passengers, the only two human beings who actually saw what happened were John Mercer, the train's engineer, and Michael O'Reilly, his fireman.

A week of downpours had melted the winter snow-pack too fast. Torrents thundered in the deep mountain gorges. All along the Denver and Salt Lake line, telegraph keys clicked out DANGER. Bridges were at risk.

Every railroad man was nervous.

As Number 1 crossed Coal Creek Bridge, John Mercer worried about Gore Canyon Trestle, ninety miles ahead. He knew that years before, the long wooden span over the Colorado River had washed out in heavy spring floods. An unlucky engineer had driven his locomotive into the fog-shrouded canyon, only to discover too late that Gore Canyon Trestle was gone. In the four-hundred-foot plunge to the raging waters below, all souls aboard had been lost.

John Mercer worked his engine upgrade into the roaring darkness of Moffat Tunnel. He had to yell to be heard. "We'll slow up west of Windy Gap! I can check Gore Canyon Trestle from there, before we cross!" O'Reilly nodded and checked his steam pressure gauge.

Suddenly, all by itself, Mercer's throttle swung to the OFF position with a thunk.

Baffled, Mercer tugged the throttle back into position, resuming speed. "Mr. O'Reilly, did you see that?" he yelled.

"See what?" O'Reilly called back. "I can't see a thing in this gloom!"

Swirling fog swept past the cab windows as they rolled out the west tunnel portal into daylight. The long down-grade of the Continental Divide lay ahead. Mercer knew he'd have to work steam and ride his air brakes all the way. The last thing he needed was a faulty throttle.

Without warning, the conductor's air whistle shrieked next to his ear. Mercer twisted from his seat and looked back to see what was wrong. Was there an emergency back there? Sudden fear rushed over him.

In the blackness of the tunnel they'd just left burned the distant headlight of another train. Mercer jerked the throttle to full steam.

"More fire, Mr. O'Reilly!" he yelled. "Somebody's on our line! Coming fast from behind!"

O'Reilly began shoveling wildly. Mercer released gritty sand onto the tracks beneath the wheels and felt his engine surge forward and gather speed down the grade.

"He's coming on at forty-five! That crazy fella will hit us!" Mercer blasted his whistle and stared back again. Out of Moffat Tunnel burst the pursuer, a huge dark engine pulling passenger cars. It sounded its whistle, wailing eerily. "He sees us!" yelled Mercer, relieved. "Now he'll slow down."

But instead, the reckless train sped up. To avoid a collision, Mercer knew he had to outrun it. "More steam, O'Reilly! He's still coming on! We'll run to the passing track at Tabernash to get out of his way!"

Barely able to hold its own against the wild locomotive, Number 1 pounded through Fraser at fifty miles an hour. Ahead, around a sweeping curve, lay Tabernash and the passing track that could save them. But as it swept into view, Mercer's heart sank. A huge coal train, dark and silent, sat on the side track in thickening fog.

Grimly, Mercer notched out the throttle again. On into the mist and wet snow they flew.

The steep rockfaces of Windy Gap loomed around them. "What about the Trestle?" cried O'Reilly, face ashen. "Mr. Mercer? What about slowing down?"

Mercer stared at him, then into stinging snow. Ahead, dense fog shrouded Gore Canyon and the Trestle.

"Can't," he replied, eyes wild. "Can't see the Trestle." He looked back at his pursuer. "Can't slow down. Got to take it at full speed."

All at once, the throttle jumped from his grip and thunked to OFF a second time. Mercer recoiled in disbelief as his engine brake iron flew back by itself and locked. The train's wheels ground sparks along the wet rails. Brakeshoe smoke roiled up from below.

In panic, O'Reilly hollered, "Mr. Mercer, we have no fire!" The pressure gauges had dropped to ZERO. Whining and shuddering, Train Number 1 ground to a halt. Then both men heard an unearthly shriek.

O'Reilly crept to the gangway and stared back. "Methinks we're about to die, Mr. Mercer," he stammered. "Look. 'Tis the Banshee. She beckons us."

At a dead stop, they waited to be struck from behind by hundreds of tons of steel traveling at fifty miles an hour.

But they felt no collision. Instead, the figure of a baleful woman raced along the cartops, shrieking something in a language they couldn't understand. Past their faces swept an engineer and a fireman, pale and determined. Ghostly passengers followed. Then all fell silent.

MOFFAT ROAD

The spectral train had vanished. All around Mercer and O'Reilly, their cab returned to life as pressure needles jumped and the brake iron clanked free. They peered forward, skin tingling. The snow had stopped. Like a quiet curtain, the fog began to lift.

Down from the cab they climbed, stumbling forward. In wonder they stared into Gore Canyon. The rails twisted out and down into nothingness. More fog blew away. Gore Canyon Trestle was completely gone.

Later, as they prepared to return to Denver, the conductor scratched his head. "How you knew this trestle was washed out, in the fog and all, beats me," he said. "Got a sixth sense, there, Mr. Mercer. All souls aboard owe you their lives."

Hardly listening, Mercer leaned close to O'Reilly. "Wasn't it twenty years ago that other train went over?" he whispered.

"In April, yup."

"April twenty-ninth, wasn't it? I think it was. O'Reilly, that's today."

O'Reilly shrugged. "A miracle, Mr. Mercer. Methinks one accident here was enough for her, maybe."

"For who?" asked the conductor, overhearing.

But O'Reilly and Mercer wordlessly turned away and swung up into the cab. A few minutes later they backed their train up the grade toward Tabernash. High above, patches of sunlight swept the peaks.

It would be a safe run back to Denver. The rains had ended.

Author's Note

Banshee comes from the Irish Gaelic words, *bean sídhe*, which mean *bean* (woman) of the *sídhe* (fairies). According to legend the banshee foretells death by wailing where it will soon take place. Irish immigrants who came to America in the nineteenth century to work on its new railroads brought stories of the banshee with them. In the days of steam locomotives, wooden trestles built over rivers sometimes collapsed without warning and people lost their lives. In this retelling of a banshee legend the fairy woman warns two trainmen, only this time her mission is one of mercy.